For
Robert Pancheri, 1916 - 1996
and Bridget Pancheri, 1918 - 1997

First published in 1999

1 3 5 7 9 10 8 6 4 2

© text and illustrations Jan Pancheri 1999

Jan Pancheri has asserted her right under
the Copyright, Designs and Patents Act, 1988,
to be identified as the author and illustrator of this work

First published in the United Kingdom in 1999 by
Hutchinson Children's Books
Random House UK Limited
20 Vauxhall Bridge Road, London SW1V 2SA

Random House Australia (Pty) Limited
20 Alfred Street, Milsons Point, Sydney
New South Wales 2061, Australia

Random House New Zealand Limited
18 Poland Road, Glenfield
Auckland 10, New Zealand

Random House South Africa (Pty) Limited
Endulini, 5A Jubilee Road, Parktown 2193, South Africa

Random House UK Limited Reg. No. 954009

A CIP catalogue record for this book is available from the British Library

ISBN: 0 09 176881 0

Printed in Singapore

The Little Angel

Jan Pancheri

HUTCHINSON

London Sydney Auckland Johannesburg

It was Christmas Eve.
The angels were
getting ready to fly
down to Earth to
take their message
of peace and
goodwill to all
mankind.

The Little Angel wanted to
go too.
   She had a special feeling
that she was needed on
Earth tonight.

But no. The bigger angels said she was too small to undertake such a long and important journey.

However, they said she could help them get ready by brushing the cobwebs from their silver wings.

The host of angels stood on the Big Cloud waiting for their guiding stars.

As the stars dropped down above their heads, the angels took off in a rush of wings.

'Goodbye!' called the Little Angel.

As she turned to go she happened to look up. There, shining above her like a diamond, was her very own star.

The Little Angel knew that she was meant
to visit Earth that night.

She took a deep breath and dived into
the darkness, thinking she would soon
catch up with the others.

But a gust of wind picked her up and sent
her off course. She found herself falling
through the night sky and through the icy
cold clouds. Down, down, down she went
until she landed, bump, on the snow.

She heard voices singing. The angel host cannot be very far away, she told herself. But the singing came from a nearby church.

'Earth is beautiful,' she said to herself.

She flew past a row of houses where Christmas trees shone from every window.

She flew above a street full of shops strung with fairy lights.

Eventually, she came to a busy market full of people rushing to buy their last-minute Christmas presents.

In a corner an old man was playing his fiddle to a small group of children. A little cat peeped out from under the folds of his coat and sniffed the tin hungrily, though there was only money inside.

It was beginning to snow again. The old man put the fiddle in the crook of his arm and the money in his pocket.

'That's all for now, children,' he said, with a wave. 'Happy Christmas!'

I am going with you, the Little Angel decided. As she followed him she saw the coins fall through a hole in his pocket. She called out to warn him, but he could not hear her.

On the way home the old man stopped by a shop to buy himself some food, but when he reached in his pocket he found he only had enough for his cat's supper.

They trudged on through the snow until they came to a dark and dingy street.

The old man stopped at one of the tumbledown houses and let himself in.

Inside there was hardly any furniture. Just a tatty old armchair and an empty fireplace.

The old man lit a candle and gave the cat food and milk.

'You're a good cat, Mishka, to keep me company all day in the cold,' he told her.

Then he dropped into the armchair and closed his eyes.

'Don't go to sleep!' cried the Little Angel. 'It's too cold for you.'

But the old man could not hear her.

She tried flapping her wings, hoping the draught would wake him. Then she blew softly on his cheek; but still he didn't stir.

I will go to the market and find food for him, and wood to make a fire, she decided.

As she went, the Little Angel put her star above the house so she would be able to find it when she returned.

The marketplace was deserted and the stalls were shut.

The Little Angel could only find leftovers: a half-empty packet of biscuits and a stale bun. She did find some logs for his fire though.

But when she tried to lift them, they would not move. Not an inch.

There was nothing for it but to go back empty-handed, for time was getting on and the night was growing colder and colder.

Her star was shining above the old man's house, but something was different.

There were trails of footprints in the snow leading to his house and his door was open. As the Little Angel got closer she could hear voices inside.

The old man's room was full of people! A fire was blazing in the grate and a child was fussing over Mishka. At first the Little Angel couldn't see the old man because there were so many people standing around him.

But when she did, she saw he was warmly wrapped in a blanket with a bowl of soup in his hands.

'We didn't know you were here,' a lady was telling him. 'But we saw a star shining above your house and that is what made us come. Otherwise we would never have found you.'

'It must have been a very lucky star,' laughed the old man.

The Little Angel smiled to herself. All at once she knew just how important her journey to Earth had been.

The people in the old man's room began to sing,
softly at first and then louder and more joyfully,
all the Christmas carols they knew.

The Little Angel took her star and flew out
the window, up and up above the snow
cloud where the angel host was waiting.

'Peace on earth,' the Little Angel sang
with them.

'And goodwill to all mankind.'